A Prince From the Sea

Gerald Ockham

Published by Gerald Ockham, 2016.

A PRINCE FROM THE SEA

First edition. March 10, 2016.

Written by Gerald Ockham.

Have you ever heard a mermaid tale? Well, of course you have, everyone has. You know the way that it goes, too. Usually it's a fisherman who's the hapless hero. Out on his boat, looking for the regular kind of catch of sardines or mackerel, he picks up something unusual when he hauls in his nets, one fine day. It's a bigger creature than his usual fish, more human sized, but with a tail that gleams with translucent blue-green scales. And a torso that shimmers with an unlikely beauty, and eyes that charm his with all the unspoken enchantments she has in her quiver full of arrows. Sometimes she takes a fancy to the fisherman, too. Perhaps enough to let him take her home, on land. Sometimes even enough to abandon her tail, and take on human limbs, however much they may make her suffer. And for a while, often, it works well enough. And then, sometimes, after a while, it stops working quite as well.

That folk-tale version doesn't really cover my own experience with the folk of the sea, the merpeople. My mermaid wasn't a mermaid at all, for starters. But then, I'm male myself, and gay. So if it had been, then there'd have been a lot less emotion and *sturm und drang* trailing in its wake. I'm also not a fisherman by trade, although I own a boat. Back in my London life, I was a bookseller in the family business – a book-store owner, in fact. But when my uncle left me a little crofter's cottage on one of the islands on the west coast of Scotland, it had been a dream come true. Enough, at least, for me to sell off the shop, and use the money to buy an annuity and follow my dream of the life of a scholar and recluse in the wilds of Scotland. Dear old Uncle Joe, he didn't just leave me the cottage, either. But also a couple of boats, fifty acres of unfarmable land, a shed, a boathouse and his rare book collection. I was in heaven for the first couple of weeks.

The boats were a) a tiny rowboat, that was fun to take out on fine days when the sea was balmy and forgiving. And highly dangerous if it was even a little bit moody, or there was a major tidal event scheduled according to the tables and radio warnings. And b) a very nice, not quite professional-level fishing boat. It was a little too advanced for my sailing experience and capabilities, but within days I was learning fast, and loving it.

So I decided to start taking it seriously. That meant fuelling up properly, and taking her out regularly, even though it didn't come cheap. Keeping everything ship-shape, as you might say – nets and decks and engine and the lot, regularly serviced and fully licensed. And for what I didn't know, I hired a retired ship's captain, on the other side of the island, to teach me. There was a hell of a lot more that I didn't know, than I'd known – paperwork, and tides, and legislation and commercial markets, making it a viable proposition instead of a dilettante's hobby. And it still thrilled me.

It took me three months for the dizzy new shine to wear off the whole venture. And by that time, it wasn't that I was sick of it, wanted to throw it up again and go home. I'd just got to the point where I was taking it properly seriously, and it wasn't something I wanted to do part-time and casually. I settled into my island cottage, and hunkered down into my new routine, and this was my life, now.

And a couple of months later my routine had become my life. Regular fishing runs were part of my week, and when I wasn't out solo, I'd schedule in runs with other pro fishermen on the island, to share in the costs and the profits. I was actually in the black with it already, and I'd never been happier. I felt more myself, in the thick of a fishing trip, than in the little mobile library job I'd picked up on the island.

It wouldn't be unreasonable for anyone reading this tale to now assume – given my lead-in – the next stage of my tale. That during the course of a trip out on the *Pretty Lady* – my boat – I'd put my nets out, had a ciggie and a snooze, and then come to myself to pull the nets in. And, in so doing, discovered that amongst the shiny wriggling fishies in my nets, I'd also caught myself one of the folk of the sea, a handsome fellow with a tail where, well, his tail should be. (Or a mermaid, of course, but I wouldn't be half so interested in that, and nor would anyone I'd be likely to tell the tale to.)

But in fact it went a little differently to the traditional narrative. It's true, though, that I was out on the fishing boat on a trip, with a catch in view and the nets in the water. It was a pleasure jaunt as well, though, because it was always a pleasure to be out there, or at least at that point it still hadn't become solely a chore. I appreciated the view from the tiller, and took a nip out of my hipflask, and it was very nice altogether. Quite a meditative experience, thinking about the beauties of nature, and the beauties of the hot young guy who'd taken over the harbour café from the old dragon of a lady who'd run it previously, too. I might be a literary old git – well, a little past forty – but only a little – and an aspiring bearded old seadog, but I still have urges. Not quite past it yet, you know. Not quite.

There was something a little different to my previous trips, though, even though it took a while for me to identify it. It was music, somewhere in the background of my appreciation of the lovely brisk day and the green rolling waves and the freeness. But then, I wasn't miles out at sea. Presumably I was hearing some concert taking place on shore. (Though it'd have to be bloody loud, even if it was a brass band in the middle of the island's tiny market town.) Or someone doing a bit of busking around the few shops dotted round the harbour, a few lonely island folk songs.

Of course I was just rationalising to myself. I wasn't a long way out, it was true. But still too far, really, to hear music so clearly, if it was onshore. Not unless I had a dog's or a bat's hearing, and at my age I didn't. But the mind persists in making sense of what's not sensible. I was too busy with some pleasant sexy daydreams, to work through a problem with any logical rigour.

But if something persists long enough, it'll impress itself on your conscious mind eventually. And when I really thought about it – or found myself thinking about it – I recognised that it was singing, not an instrument. Still I didn't process it, didn't admit that a human voice couldn't possibly carry so far, not unless it was a big fat operatic professional soprano. Maybe I assumed someone in the village had professional talent, and stuck themselves in this lonely Scottish backwater for much the same reasons as myself. (Romantic disappointment, and misanthropy, and a love of nature and books and calling your time your own.)

It was utterly daft, as a hypothesis, or perhaps I was. But it was the best explanation that I had, as I squinted into the sun from behind my dark glasses, a little over-heated in my woolly sweater. (Knitted by the lady who ran the only newsagents on the island.) My boots were thick and heavy, ungiving on my poor feet. At least there was a breeze, though. It lifted long strands of my dark hair, slightly greying now, and in need of a barbering. The only man handy with a pair of hairdresser's scissors on the island opened up shop twice a week at the island market, and I'd let it go too long in the meantime. Normally I prided myself on being quite dapper, even if not in my prime any more. But if I let this carry on, I'd be a proper island wild-man.

So I only paid enough attention to allow the music to enhance the bob of the waves and the pretty horizon, and I was miles away, simply miles. So much

so, that when some noise broke me out of my wool-gathering, I wasn't even sure
what it had been. Then it came again, and turned out to have been a loud gnaw-
ing creak. It had me gaping about myself, looking for the source of it. But I saw
nothing, and decided it must simply have been a plank that was a little water-
logged and less than true anymore. Not to worry, I thought, with the sun on my
face. Not to worry.

After a moment there must have been some native logic, working deep deep
down inside the well of my subconscious, though, that decided to contradict my
easy assumptions. Rehearsing it over in my mind, I discovered that I was quite
sure that the creak had come from the starboard of the boat. Well over to starboard, in fact. And a little behind me. So I turned around, and I had a look in
that direction.

It was worth having taken the look, going by the results. I was being boarded,
it appeared. Or at least, my little boat was. A handsome young man was trying to
lever himself up and over the side, giving me a rather impressive view of his pecs
and all the rest as he did so, sweating and possibly grunting a bit.

Part of the reason I got such a good, and thorough view, was that he was
naked. Or, at least, the half of him I could see as he struggled, that half was quite
starkers. It was a bit of a shocker. He was busy wrestling with the lip of the rail,
as I first looked at him. But then he looked up, and at me, as I swore. He had the
most beautiful blue-green eyes.

You'd think he'd look shame-faced, a pirate caught red-handed like that. But
no, he grinned at me, quite as bold as brass. The rest of him was just as beautiful
as his eyes, too. His hair was reddish and too long, and all the lovelier for being
a bit too long, and everything about his tone and muscle and bone was perfectly
proportioned and subtle and dazzling, and frankly–. Well. I'll restrain myself, a
bit. It had been a while.

Yes, I'll leave it there. You get the general picture, I'm sure. And also, it wasn't
even the most interesting thing about him, or about the whole tableau. What
happened next had my jaw dropped open about ready to hit the deck, and hit it
hard. Because he successfully hauled himself up, arms popping with flexed muscle, and flipped himself over the side of the boat, exactly the way he'd obviously been trying to do. Perhaps I should have run up to him and shoved him back
overboard, the instant I laid eyes on him. But there's something about someone

doing something so outrageously transgressive, and doing it with a cheeky grin and looking right into your eyes as they do it. It's disarming, to say the least.

That wasn't what did it, though – what had me stunned, eyes popping with wonder and a worried wondering about if my brain had finally softened irreparably, one too many pints of mild down at the harbour bar, too many red-faced arguments about politics and the correct way to put a net out with a forecast of high winds and dangerous currents. I certainly was stunned, though. I fainted. So would you, if the bottom half of a handsome young man turned out to be a tail.

I knew I'd fainted – however many minutes later – due to the fact that I was coming out of it. My head was hurting and I had the deck of the boat swaying under my back, the sun gone in and the sky looking a darker, angry blue overhead. I wasn't alone, either. I clearly hadn't imagined the beautiful young pirate who'd been making a felonious entry on my sweet little vessel. He was still right there beside me – looking down at me with a very sincere, concerned look on his face. He had one hand on my cheek, and the other on my chest, or resting on my chest through my Arran sweater. His face was quite gentle. That was definitely the guy. Fortunately, even if he had shocking morals, and was intending burglary as part of his assault on my property, it didn't seem as if he was the violent type.

He still had a tail, though. I hadn't imagined that, either.

He wasn't quite as enigmatic as I remembered him, pre-faint. In fact, he actually spoke to me, and he had a lovely voice too. Unfortunately not one that spoke in English, or in any language that I recognised. But lovely, just the same. Do merpeople usually speak English? I suppose it's quite unlikely. I don't think they come under the jurisdiction of the Crown or Commonwealth. I was grateful for the concern he was transparently expressing, in any case. So grateful, that I felt minded to return the civility, and offer him some refreshments.

Perhaps he wasn't ideally constructed to take afternoon tea with the vicar, it was true. And I was still wondering, halfway, if I'd taken a more severe knock to the head than I knew about, and was only dreaming this very strange development. And yet, to the best of my perceptions, it was real enough, and there seemed no alternative, real or dreaming, but to settle in and deal with circumstances as I found them. I offered him hot coffee, made Irish out of my hipflask because I thought that I, at least, could do with it. And some slightly tired sandwiches out of my lunchbox. Though he couldn't precisely communicate his opinions or thanks on the subject, he seemed pleased. At least, to judge by the big smile on his face, and his vigorous nods in my direction. I did speculate that perhaps neither were exactly what he was used to, as dietary staples. But it didn't seem to put him off one bit, and he made magnificent inroads into the sandwiches at a speed that was truly impressive.

Perhaps I should have been calling the cops, or the alienists, or the island medical service, I don't know. But after he'd picked me up and tended to my wounds – well, after a fashion – it felt as if it would have been a bit uncivil, and over the top. I had, after all, no evidence of nefarious intent. Perhaps he just liked to pay afternoon visits to the island's fishermen, from one lover of a good plate of haddock or a nice kipper to another. What with the lack of a common language, conversation was a difficulty, as we sat and chewed and took the odd swig. But we managed well enough, socially – pointing at the pretty view, and nodding over the excellence of my cream cheese and smoked salmon rolls, and grinning at the cheek of the gulls who tried to nick the odd crumb here and there.

In fact it was a lot of fun, even despite the fact that we didn't have a word of any language in common, barring pointing at items of food and equipment on the boat, and grunting out naming terms. It passed the time, but it wasn't even the primary thing holding my attention. My, but he was pretty, even with his lower half covered in shiny silver scales. Oh, well, I think it was reasonable. I may be a little the wrong side of forty – depending which side you're looking from. But I'm still a healthy and interested gay male, with the motor still running if someone takes the trouble to pull on the cord. It was a perfectly natural response. You'd have had to take a good look at him to understand. Those eyes were really delightful, and as for his shoulders, his abs...

Maybe I was a little bit over excited. But I was still monitoring the basic essentials, like the weather and the time of day and the tides and currents. Even though I was having quite a surprising – astounding – nice time, reluctantly and eventually these factors came together, and I knew it was time to call a halt to visiting hours. I made as much obvious to my guest – and it wasn't altogether an easy job, with very little in the way of actual words to rely on. But once I did put the general gist of the thing across, he didn't prove quite as cooperative as I'd fondly expected, despite being a little reluctant myself to let him go.

And that was a little bit of an understatement, too. Instead, I was gripped – not harshly, not violently, but still gripped – by the wrists, and pulled forward much closer to him. Not into his arms, exactly – although that would have been quite exciting, proper bodice-ripper material. But very nearly, and forcibly enough so that I couldn't help but notice what nice hands he had, strong and long-fingered and only very slightly webbed, in a rather elegant way. And now he was talking at me, with his handsome broad-cheekboned face up rather close, and his lovely blue-green eyes sparklingly bright and dancing. There we were, crouched together, me with my legs splayed out in tired old jeans, and his tail glinting with dancing silver lights in the sunlight, and his beautiful soft-lipped mouth gabbing away at a hundred miles a minute.

Of course, just because he was talking, didn't mean that I understood a word of what it was that he was so earnestly telling me. Gestures, expressions and intonations were much more useful. He gestured out at the horizon as he spoke, at the grey-blue expanse of the sea. And he grimaced in a way that told its own tale. Then he pointed to the island – then he pointed in my direction – and then he waggled my hand a bit, by the wrist, and he smiled at me so beautifully... I'm not saying that it didn't influence my decision a bit. I'm a single guy, and it had been a while since – anything, and this beautiful young creature was the most seductive thing I'd laid eyes on in a good long while. There weren't many gay bars, on this little Scottish island. Or any, in fact. And I'd never had that much luck back in my mainland life, either. Too fussy, perhaps. Or too much of an oddity. Academic, and a bit shy, and earnest, not so much the clubbing and casual hook-ups type.

It wasn't that I didn't get the gist of what it was he was saying to me. He didn't fancy an immediate return to his native waters, then. Instead, he wanted to come visit with me. Maybe for dinner, or maybe for a one-nighter, or even for a longer stay. Maybe for good. Whichever option it was he was trying to get at, I would probably have resolved myself against it. On the grounds that I was a sensible middle-aged writer and sailor and single guy. I wasn't to be wooed by pretty sea-green eyes and a swishy silver tail, wielded by someone who'd boarded my boat without an invite. Who'd promptly ingratiated himself enough to inveigle tea and sandwiches out of me, instead of being tossed overboard. He opened his mouth again, though, and this time it was to sing.

And now I knew where the singing I'd heard earlier had come from. That was it, exactly the thin pure eerie voice that I'd heard, much too delicate and seductive to be a mighty roar heard from the island itself. He didn't exactly give me the benefit of a full aria. It was just a minute or two of wordless music from his vocal cords, or at least no words that were intelligible to me. It made me feel tipsy, and dreamlike, and completely seduced when he'd barely laid a hand on me, or not more than that at least. Oh hell, why wouldn't I invite him home?

I don't think that he was a literal Circe, the kind of merman or mermaid who in legend combed their hair with sly and malignant intent on the lethal rocks, singing to draw men in and break their little boats. Apart from anything else, he seemed rather keener on going home to the island harbour and docking my little craft nice and safely, rather than doing her any injury. I wasn't hypnotised, as such. But I was very much charmed. It was delightful to find out that my fishy new companion wasn't only aesthetically blessed – and he was certainly the prettiest thing I'd seen in many a long dry month. But also to be musical, to have a voice like that? I was very much a music buff, as well as a reader, a writer and a sailor. A little more time with this strange and gifted charmer was a gift I couldn't pass on.

It would have been difficult, in any case. He was so absolutely set on the idea.

It was quite simple to decide on the matter, then. But not quite so simple to actually accomplish it. The simple fact of his unusual anatomy ensured that. Getting into harbour wasn't an issue, but once the boat was moored we were a bit stuck. I was only glad that the place was deserted on a late weekday afternoon, for once. (All the old soaks of the island no doubt getting soaked further, in the harbour pub.) I wasn't going to give up. Not just because it presented a bit of a challenge, though. There had to be some way or another. For a moment I considered borrowing a wheelbarrow from my neighbour, Arthur, who had a smallholding and seemingly limitless amounts of equipment in his sheds. On the other hand, Arthur might want to know what I wanted it for. And once he knew, he might want to help. He wasn't the most discreet person I knew, especially after a couple of single malts. It didn't seem like the best idea.

But I wasn't going to worry in any case, because I'd already decided that I was going to find a way around it, and that was that. "You need a name," I decided, one foot on the lip of the side of the boat as I readied myself to jump onto the dock. "I can't just keep calling you 'you', and quivering every time you bat your pretty lashes at me." He smiled very sweetly in response, looking up at me where he was posed like a coy semi-nude model in the hull of the boat. It was so knowing and mock-innocent that I'd have sworn he knew exactly what I was saying. His nipples were perky in the sharp breeze, and there was just the slightest hint of stubble on his immaculate jawline, and he had to know just how lovely he was.

"I'll call you Pos – short for Poseidon, since that's the only sea-god I can remember." I blinked at him, and felt a little dizzy. The only way I could take this was in the most phlegmatic way possible, as if it was perfectly everyday to pick up a merman out of the waves. But every so often I got a wincing little blast of unreality, and had to wonder, for a moment, about my sanity. Or otherwise.

He raised an eyebrow, now, and looked quite sceptical. I suppose at the name, or at my comment on his eyelashes. "Oh, yes," I said, firmly. "I need a name for you – and if you're not giving me an alternative, then Pos will do, subject to later alteration." He rolled his eyes at this, and grinned, but I got no argument out of him, or other suggestions, however incomprehensible. So I figured we were going with Pos. "Now, Pos," I said breezily. "If you're coming home for dinner – and it does look as if you've invited yourself – then we need to figure out the logistics of how to get you into the back of my van. Which may be easier said than done, in the absence of a winch and haulage gear, but I'm sure we can manage it someway or somehow." I was fairly confident. I've played pub footie, and worked out on and off over the years, and if I say so myself, I've still not really let myself go to seed. Under the woolly sweaters and old-geezer corduroys, I still have quite a fine torso, if anyone bothered to look these days.

My confidence was justified, in the end, because one way and another, we persevered, and we achieved the task. I don't mean to imply by that, that it wasn't exceedingly tricky, because it certainly was. I had cause to be thankful for the lengths of rope in the back of my van, formerly used to drag safety equipment into the hold of the boat. There was also extensive use of a sliding panel segment nicked off an absent friend's boat nearby, and considerable effort and burning of solid muscle fibres on both our parts, before we actually managed to get Pos both onto dry land, and into my vehicle. And yet we managed it, and as much credit due to Pos as myself, for the outcome. He certainly was determined to have a proper social evening out in the human world, judging by the effort he was willing to put into making it happen.

Once we'd got him in there, via our joint efforts, though, things were vastly simpler. (And a tremendous relief, it was, to have him safely behind the van doors, banged shut, and away from the eyes of any passing interested islander. It wasn't as if we were committing any crime. It would just have been very hard to explain, barring to anyone straying out of the pub completely blotto.) And he seemed quite pleased to be in there, chirping at me from the back and sliding up the black vinyl I had laid on the floor, to distract me thoroughly while driving. Then once we arrived at my little cottage it was a matter of putting the whole procedure in reverse, and labouring to haul him indoors as quickly as might be practical. My neighbour's wheelbarrow did actually come in useful at this point. With no necessity of an explanation for borrowing it, since he was fortunately out at the time.

It wasn't as if our troubles were over, once we'd got him indoors, though. There was still the matter of getting him re-located to the bathroom, since it seemed like the only and obvious spot. (My kitchen sink wasn't nearly big enough, and the bidet would hardly have been comfortable.) It seemed to be becoming a matter of urgency, because by the looks of them, his scales were showing the effects of dehydration. They were dulling and losing their beautiful sheen, and also their smooth glassy finish, even beginning to peel and distort a bit at the edges. He didn't actually look unwell, beyond that, but if it was the canary in the mine, the first sign of ill effects, then I certainly didn't want to be the unwitting cause of more serious illness in my unusual guest. Hydration was certainly key at this point.

But even that we did manage. Mostly, probably, because the uncle who'd left me the cottage had had considerable mobility issues, and so had had a downstairs bathroom installed, including a walk-in bath with handy grips and handles. I hardly dare to think about the issues involved if that hadn't been the case. As well as the wheelbarrow, of course.

It still took a little labour to get Pos – as I was still calling him – actually into the bath. But his reaction to the sight of it was positive, and he was cooperative about getting in there and getting the water running. Indeed he seemed already familiar with the general idea of taps and running water, which had me speculating for a minute or two, before more reprehensibly lusty speculations took over. Well, he was getting soaked, and wet, and it was very fetching on him, splashing around like that.

It was quite fun, in the end, to blast the taps and get the bath full, even though I couldn't help being a bit shy about it. Shyer than Pos was, at least. He was clearly having a good time, and urged me on when I was dubious about applying a dollop of bath foam to the tap end. It seemed an unnatural human product to be mixing with a wild creature of the sea, and it wasn't as if he wasn't already looking a bit the worse for wear. But Pos was insistent, and then delighted at the foamy, pine-scented end results. He was quickly playing and blowing with the bubbles resulting, and then gave himself a quick foam beard and moustache, winking as he modelled the end results for me, and set me laughing.

It didn't seem like an obvious, blatant attempt at seduction. But whether it was intended that way or not, it was still pretty effective, I thought wistfully. (Although surely any seductive approaches would be rendered null and void, I also pointed out mentally, given the basic restrictions of merman anatomy. Very unfortunately.) Better not to think about that too much, since too much pondering on the subject could only lead to frustration and embarrassment. Instead I got up and went to seek out tea and nourishment for Pos, as a guest in my little home. I explained by miming the procedures of eating and drinking, which I assumed would get the general idea across. But I wasn't sure about how successful it was. Not judging by the raised eyebrows and giggles he met my efforts with.

I wasn't sure exactly what was being implied here, but it was certainly enough to make me a little shy. I got out of there quick, and once in the kitchen, I distracted myself by focusing firmly upon what to offer the guest lurking in my bathtub. Some smoked salmon and rye crackers seemed like a decent idea. Surely fish would be a firm favourite of his? (If he didn't consider it unacceptably cannibalistic, but I thought it was probably possible to worry too much about offending delicate sensibilities.) And after considering brewing up a nice pot of filter coffee, for a moment, I decided against it. Instead I reached up to the top cupboard where the less frequently-required condiments were kept, and grabbed the bottle of vodka that was pushed around into the darkest corner. Maybe adding booze to this already rather flirty and awkward situation wasn't a brilliant move. But on the other hand, I felt flustered enough that a stiff drink was extremely attractive, at this point.

It needed a mixer – unless I was finally going to give in and go full time, dedicated dipsomaniac. And as I was searching out the tonic, and breaking out the ice, I thought about the last time I'd hung out with my sister's kid, Alan, shortly before I'd moved to the island. He was a good kid, deep into his graduate studies in sociological analysis, and so much more overtly, blatantly gay than myself that you had to wonder if there's something to the genetic theory of orientation. (Not that the family's only rich in inverts. There are also plenty of oddballs, eccentrics and golfers, and it's the last bunch who cause the most strife and arguments at family gatherings.) We'd spent a couple of hours at a sports bar – my team was playing, since I'm not a *golfer*, for Christ's sake. And after a couple of shots and two refined and obscure microbrews, Alan had decided it was time to lecture his maiden-aunt old bachelor uncle on the perils of standardised social expectations of male homosexual sexuality. (Christ knows I didn't ask him to. Is no-one decently repressed any more? At his age, I couldn't have uttered the phrase 'male homosexual sexuality' to anyone of my parents' generation, not without dying of heat-loss through excess blushing.) It started off, his lecture, as very cultured and educated, lots of references to obscure French structuralist philosophers and knowing pop-culture winks. And – after a couple more drinks – it degenerated into cries of, "It's not all about the arse!" And, even, "Or about the dick, even!"

Thanks, Alan. I think perhaps the boy thought I was a repressed virgin who needed assisting out of his repressed shell. The poor deluded kid.

But maybe it was my own fault – I'd bought him the drinks, after all, what with him being a poor penniless grad student. And then the education of his Tragic Uncle never stopped – relentless explanations of the fact that, popular assumptions to the contrary, there was more to sex than penetration, for girls and gay guys both. It wasn't that any of his crashing, spectacular, obvious insights were anything new to me. He was totally teaching granny – or Uncle – to suck eggs, despite him thinking he'd discovered America, or something along those lines. The memory just came back to me now. It seemed relevant to current circumstances, I suppose.

And the memory – the lecture, and the ideas involved – led to trains of thought that had me blushing reluctantly, as I returned with a tray, weighted down with snacks and drinks. I firmly tried to put those thoughts away, as Pos greeted me quite unintelligibly, but with clear pleasure and a broad, sweet smile. (As well as a languid stretch and flex, that looked utterly casual and unintentionally erotic. Unintentional, my arse, I thought, though. There was a glint in his eye as he finished – yawning and fluttering his eyelashes – that spoke of a complete, satisfied awareness of what he was doing. And its effects, too.) Of course, the bubble-bath assisted in protecting his modesty, as he stretched. Well, up to a point, at least.

He'd given himself a little crown of bubbles, somehow – either deliberately, or unconsciously by accident. Going by his serene and unconscious air, I opted for the latter, and it was deeply unconsciously comical. It really did look like a little crown, and it was hilarious, and rather fetching, too.

And he beamed up at me – naked as any fishy, and with the bubbles surrounding purely decorative in value – as I offered him salmon and vodka. We toasted each other, myself in English, and he had some benevolent cry that was presumably approximately equivalent to 'Bottoms up!' or some such. I took it that way in any case, although it might equally well have meant, 'A curse on your house, and immediate open war declared upon you and yours!' But he drank off the vodka in one gulp, and didn't cough nor even water a little around the eyes. It was something else, to be frank, that seemed rather suspiciously familiar and natural to him. Or perhaps mermen had their own stills, which would be very handy for them, if rather hard to imagine the practical technicalities of.

And, drink downed, he concentrated – well, not so much on the salmon, which I might have expected. Oh, he nibbled at it politely – and at least he wasn't offended by the fishy offering. But most of his attention, to tell the truth, seemed to be directed my way. And it made me a little self-conscious and uncomfortable, to be honest. If someone had put the thumbscrews on me, I would have had to admit, hand on heart, that there was something a little bit suggestive in that aquamarine gaze. I mean, perhaps I was flattering myself. I've accounted myself, quite frankly, as knocking on a bit. On the other hand, I was also accounted a bit of a looker in my younger years, and even myself, I don't think that I scrubbed up too badly then. Black hair, blue eyes, quite nice cheekbones, reasonably well-built from soccer and semi-pro martial arts... Those were the days. And, going by this young fella's eyes on me, those days might not be altogether gone yet. It was a bit of a shock, though, when he leaned forward – and rested a cheek on his hand, to gaze at me the more soulfully, head on the side of the bath – and began to sing, that damn elusive song of the sea again.

Maybe those days really weren't gone. My dissolute youth felt less and less distant all the time, no matter what my dear patronising nephew might think.

Well, I might be right or I might be wrong. But I was a little bit stressed and freaked out either way, and I flinched a little backwards and away from the bathtub. Not out of aversion, but more out of a mistrust of my own judgement. (And my own desires, perhaps. I wasn't any spring chicken, and I really didn't want to be making a fool of myself, making a move on someone inappropriately young – well, early to mid-twenties, in any case – and being rejected. And possibly laughed at.) I wasn't the only one in motion, though. Pos sprung up out of the bath, right as I stepped back. And his hand closed – tight – on my arm.

Not enough to leave marks, mind you. Well, perhaps only a little bit. But enough to pull me closer, instead of letting me back away. He was up very close, now, enough that we were eye to eye, and it felt like my breathing was being positively strangled. His fingers massaged my arm as he held me there – and he was wonderfully strong. Even with his build I wouldn't have guessed at it. It must have taken incredible core strength just to maintain uprightness in that pose, what with having a fish tail instead of legs. And he couldn't tell me what he wanted, or what he wanted to say, of course. But somehow he managed to put it all into his eyes, and to make me blush doing it. There was still that little crown of foam on his head, and it made me wonder if he was royalty, amongst his own kind. He certainly had that air of entitlement, as if he was usually accorded *droit de seigneur*, and expected it, too.

And there was something hot about it. Isn't there always something hot about confidence? Or arrogance, even. I should probably have known better, but I felt like he'd made the first move, and that justified a little foolishness on my own part. I let myself drift a little bit closer – even though I was a little painfully aware, that the light of the high window was probably lighting up the silver in my black hair, where it wasn't quite so black any more. And Pos slid a finger into the collar of my sensible button-down shirt, and let it tug down at the first button, as if there was some problem with it. Or some problem with it being still buttoned. Well, wasn't I the host, and he the guest? If there was something that displeased him, then wasn't it my role to take care of it?

I pulled away from him again – and it took a little force to do it. But this time, I wasn't just backing away out of timidity and uncertainty, out of the desire not to look a fool. Instead I started – a little hesitantly – to unbutton my shirt. And I was only egged on, by the long exhale of hot breath out of his mouth as he watched me. It spoke more eloquently than words could have done, in any language. I peeled off my cosy sweater, my shirt, everything else, the lot. His eyes on me were all the encouragement I could desire. I know perfectly well I'm not as past-it and aesthetically diminished as I like to describe myself, not such an old museum piece. But caution and uncertainty make it an easy role to play, when you've been burned once too often out there in the meat-market of love and romantic disillusionment. I didn't feel old, or past it, or undesirable, under his gaze.

And if he was going to watch – and to reach out, but I stayed out of reach, teasing a little – then I might as well give him a show. I made a slow epic of it. The way I'd almost forgotten how to do, forgotten that I could do, at this point. (It had been a long time, since the last time.) I almost forgot that I was stripping for one of the merfolk, if I hadn't lost my mind and wasn't only hallucinating. That he'd boarded my vessel without permission, was a reprehensible pirate I should have shoved overboard and thought no more on. Except I didn't forget it, because in fact the thought was excruciatingly hot, erotic in the extreme.

I could have wished for something more exotic to show, outerwear discarded, than plain black long-leg briefs and a white T-shirt. But then again, thank God for it. A thong really wouldn't have suited me, and it wasn't as if I could have carried it off with a straight face. He seemed pleased enough with what he saw – and grabbed at – and even those last scraps of modesty were dispensed with quick enough. He let himself slide down into the foam, as I peeled them off. And his hands were suspiciously out of sight, as my own popped buttons and pushed at soft cotton. At least I knew for sure that I had nothing to be embarrassed about in what I was revealing. My exercise routine might not be strenuous, but it was adequate, strict and regular, and my body was nothing that needed covering up.

And I gave it some extra verve to finish off with, throwing my pants and vest so that they had a soft crash-landing in the linen-basket. (Well, in fact, I missed with the vest, but I plead that it wasn't my best shot, and I was severely distracted at the time.) It distracted me enough that Pos managed to lunge out and get a grip on me where I hadn't let him up until this point. And he was very insistent about pulling me up to the bath, and his eyes were hot and excited, and I could not resist. I could not.

I didn't know exactly what to expect. But I repeated to myself all of those lecture bullet points that dear Alan had bellowed out into the smoky air of a deserted bar, months back, about satisfaction being more than ejaculation, and such-like. And in any case I dispensed with thinking. I just climbed into the bath with him – blushing and shy like a virgin, almost. And when he pushed me down into the bubbles and loomed over me, tail thrashing and water slopping out over the sides, I swear that I felt about nineteen, ready to be deflowered. His mouth on my nipples made me whimper a little. It was merciless and bordering on painful, and still tinglingly hot and hardening my dick. And then, when his head disappeared under the water and the suds, I gasped for air and could not close my mouth against my moans, not to save my life.

Why hadn't it occurred to me that he could breathe underwater? True, there'd been no obvious sign of gills at his neck or cheeks. But that didn't mean that they weren't there. Just that they were *discreet*. He was one of the merfolk, after all. Of course he could breathe underwater. When his head bobbed up – from where it was travelling down, down the trail of hair on my chest, to between my legs – I saw the gills, little red ducts venting out into the water from the side of his neck. Very pretty, really, and then I stopped thinking at all, as I felt his mouth slide down onto my cock.

• • • •

JUDGING BY THE LIGHT, or absence of it, it was a fair old time later when I woke up, face down in my bed. I was vague and warmly muzzy, in the moments after waking, the usual way. My memories were unclear. And then I got clear, and smiled into my pillow. All of my body felt exhausted and very, very relaxed, and it was fantastic. It had been a very long time, longer than I'd realised, and I'd really needed what Pos had done for me. And done, and done, and done some more... There were some things he was extremely expert with, including human male anatomy and functions.

It did take a couple of minutes to really wake up properly, though. And once I had, I began to wonder. To wonder what I was doing in bed, for a start. And how, exactly, I'd gotten there in the first place. We hadn't got as drunk as all that. A little merry, but certainly not really blotto, nothing that would have had me not knowing full well what I was doing. And the sexual shenanigans, while amazing, weren't likely to have induced amnesia or unconsciousness or blackout, either. And the last option – well, it wasn't as if Pos could have picked me up out of the bath, sleepy and euphoric, and simply carried me here. He simply didn't have the minimum equipment required – though he'd proven himself more than adequate in other respects.

I'd have thought over these mysteries and revelations a lot more thoroughly, too. Except that just as I was really digging into them, there was a fresh development to consider. Namely, that although I'd assumed I was alone – since even if I'd mysteriously made it here myself, how could I have dragged a fishman along to bed with me? - it turned out that I wasn't. I could tell, by the great muscular arm that slung itself over my hip, from where I was laid turned to the wall and in a semi-foetal position.

It wasn't that I had a problem with this new development, either. No, as far as it went, it was very nice indeed, and in fact to be encouraged. And Pos elaborated upon it and continued further, kissing my neck and shoulders in a way that made me sigh and quiver quite a lot, rather embarrassingly responsive to his displays of affection. I couldn't understand what he was actually doing here, mind you, nor how precisely he'd got here. But what he was doing here, now that he was? That was a-okay, and even more than that. The thing I hadn't been expecting, though, was the limb that joined the arm slung over me, trapping my calves as it swung over my legs.

It was a leg. A leg.

A leg! *What the hell is going on*, is what my response was to that. I jumped about a mile, and dragged myself out from under all the stray spare limbs that seemed to be going begging suddenly around the place. And as I did so, I rolled myself around, to look at what spider it was that had crawled all over me with its excess limbs. But it was simply Pos, of course. The same Pos I'd had a lovely sensual sexy bath with, the one I'd met this same day, the one who'd illicitly boarded my boat and seduced me into feeding him and taking him home. That one, yes. The one who'd then taken me to bed – to my bed – probably. Who else? Especially since he now seemed to be equipped with the full complement of legs.

I was amazed, and I defy anyone to say it wasn't quite reasonable to be so. I gaped at his legs quite openly, my jaw dropped. Then I looked at them, and looked at him, and at them and back again, making it pretty pointed. "How about you explain yourself, here?" I asked. "Last time I checked, you had a tail, and no legs. And now? What's going on with the legs, Pos? How come the legs?" Maybe I made it a little bit more sarcastic than necessary. But I think it was justified. That was a hell of a shock to spring on someone, quite unsuspecting.

So Pos looked down where I was looking, at a pair of fine strong muscular-thighed legs, that I'd have looked at twice on anyone. But especially on a merman, where they surely very little belonged. That wasn't the only place he was looking, though. It was between his legs, the source of his knowing and smug grin, I think. But it wasn't his newly gifted cock I was talking about. Even though I'd sneaked a perfectly natural look at that, too. And he looked up again, and winked at me.

The wink said everything, I think. 'What about it' and 'Pretty nice, huh?' and 'Well, what now?'

They were all good questions, and I thought about them earnestly. It *was* pretty nice. I wasn't sure why I should be so freaked out by it. I was already bedded – or bathed – by a merman, after all. Him acquiring a dick and a pair of legs was just... well, a bonus, really. "Well, lucky you," I agreed. "Or lucky me, even. It is just a matter of willpower, then? Or magic, or proximity to a human with legs himself?... Or set off by sexual activity?" Maybe that was it. Presumably it had happened to him before, at least. He didn't seem in the least surprised by the development, certainly.

But however much he understood, or otherwise, of my questions and comments, Pos didn't seem inclined to give me any definitive answers. Only to smile at me gently, sweetly, and to edge a little closer, offering his warmth. And probably more, judging by the encounter we'd already had. I couldn't help letting my eyes linger a little again, not just on his legs but on the other surprise he'd sprung on me. He didn't miss me looking, either. And he grinned at me, as he fondled the sea-monster between his new legs. Which was both impressive, and alert and solidly ready for all kinds of uses and fun. He didn't need to actually say so, in any language. It was very clear where his thoughts were tending.

We were both doing too much thinking, though. I abandoned thinking, and climbed aboard that perfect surprising cock. Anything else would have been a waste of an opportunity, and anyhow it was my turn to please him. He'd pleased me so much already, and so selflessly, this prince of the sea, this merfolk pirate, that I figured I owed him. I rode him to exhaustion, and then I fell asleep again, warm and sore and pleased beside him.

• • • •

SO I WOKE A SECOND time, and the light was almost gone. It had to be a fair bit later. I rubbed my eyes, and reached for Pos. Worrying, really, that it was an automatic instinct, so quickly. He wasn't there. The sheets were disordered, and the room was cold, and he wasn't there. It made my stomach sink, made me feel a little sick. Although obviously I should have expected it. So I steeled myself to accept facts, got up and put on sweatpants and my t-shirt, and took a look around the house. Yes, he was gone. Not still up walking on two legs, not back fish-tailed in the bath, not making tea in the kitchen or watching TV in the living room.

I have to admit that my cynicism kicked in at this point, and I made a much quicker check of everything I had of value in the house. Wallet, bank cards, sound system, computer, *et cetera et cetera*. But they were all still in place, and I had to laugh at myself a little. What use would a merman have, for consumer goods, considering where he was going to finally return? I felt a little embarrassed, and ashamed. It had been a fairly crass assumption, after all. He might have been a pirate of sorts, boarding my boat, but not one intent on pillage. You just get to a certain age, and it gets to be surprising if someone takes an immediate fancy to you, in that way. Although not so surprising if they up and disappear, after a single day or night together.

But I tried not to kick myself too hard, or to regret the whole episode too much. It had given me pleasure, and fun, and cause to doubt my sanity, at points. (I really should have got some decent photos of Pos while I'd had him there, but too late now.) As long as I hadn't let myself take it too seriously, become too charmed by a delightful creature who passed through my life for a few hours and shared a little erotic heat and pleasure, then, well, no harm done. (I hadn't. I hadn't, had I?)

All I needed to do was to cherish a bizarre and rather lovely memory, and keep my mouth shut. (Unless I really wanted to spend some time on the local mental ward.) And to be more careful in future, about what crawled over the side of my boat and got welcomed into my life, my boat, my bed. I could get worse than a little whiplash from a muscular thrashing tail, next time. I might get my heart broken.

· · · ·

AND I THOUGHT THAT was that, with what felt like good reason. I went to bed that night alone, and the next night too, and the next week. After that long, and a week longer, my memories of my encounter with Pos grew more and more uncertain. Not that they weren't still intense, detailed, erotic. They were, for sure. But they also began to feel unreliable and hallucinatory. Wouldn't anyone begin to doubt their memories and their own mind, after an experience like that, with no subsequent confirmatory episodes? I did, inevitably, begin to doubt it had actually happened. But I didn't freak out too much about it. A brief psychotic episode isn't all that uncommon – I found out, given the usual bouts of anxious hypochondriacal internet research. And, apparently, if it's a matter of only a solitary single experience, it's not necessarily too serious. (I wasn't too sure that my GP would agree with the opinions of unqualified internet persons, but the advice was comforting and I intended to stick with it.) And in any case, it wasn't as if I really believed that my memories were just delusions. It was only lip-service paid to rationality, out of a vague sense of grown-up duty. Really, deep down, I was certain it had been real.

I had been too sore, for a day or two after, for anything else.

But I couldn't help a few misgivings, whatever my deepest convictions. But I held on to them tightly, no matter what. And then, I started to have experiences that put the whole question out of my mind. Health-related issues, you could say. Multiple symptoms, one of them after another after another piling up, and taking up more and more space in my mind. Water retention, and curious abdominal cramps, and swollen ankles. Constipation, and cravings for the oddest food combinations. Nausea, mostly in the mornings – that was the worst. That was bad, and only got worse.

My doctor could make nothing of it, but assured me there was no serious malady that he could track down. The assurance did nothing to make me feel any better.

And then I noticed that I was putting on weight. It was persistent, no matter what I ate. (And no matter how bizarre it was.) And then, a couple of months further on, there was the first time I felt something distinctly moving, deep in my belly. It wasn't gas, and it wasn't cramps, and it wasn't anything I could identify, or wanted to. I held onto denial very strongly. But I had to wonder if sex with Pos had passed on to me some bizarre marine STD. Was it some kind of parasite? I cringed at the thought of trying to explain the circumstances leading up to *that*, with any doctor.

I fretted about it frantically, for about forty-eight hours. And then, the third day – or night, rather – I couldn't sleep for worrying. And also due to general discomfort. Because none of my other symptoms were letting up, either. In fact there were new and interesting variants adding themselves to the list all the time. Currently a raging backache was the foremost amongst them, and in the end I simply couldn't lie there, constantly shifting position to no avail, and bear it any longer. It wasn't as if my mind could settle, either.

But it was the middle of the night, and my options for taking my mind off my troubles were limited. I felt too unbearably confined indoors to sit in the living room and watch television or catch up on the internet, or do my paperwork, perish the thought. Sitting out on the lawn furniture in my garden would be perishing cold, and dull into the bargain. The boat, on the other hand, I had ready moored in the harbour. It offered distraction and escape, and enough occupation to take my mind off my body, my delusions and my reckless sexual idiocy. Oh, and being seduced, charmed and abandoned by a supernatural creature of the seas – a pretty naiad who seemed to have no intention of ever coming back for a visit.

So I got myself down there, PDQ, and felt happier the moment I set foot aboard. Not quite ecstatic, mind you – it didn't ease my backache, the walk, not as much as I'd have expected. And all the rest of the symptoms were still present and correct, too. But still, gently bobbing out of the harbour, I felt a bit better – a bit less sick – for the fresh sea air and the waves beneath me. Although the jabbing movements in my belly seemed worse, if anything. But with the boat to sail, it took my mind off it a bit, at least. I started to wonder about IBS, or appendicitis. Whatever my doc said, surely there had to be some rational physical explanation?

I ruminated on it, huddled up in the cabin for ten minutes with the tiller set to automatic and the engine puttering quietly. All of my thoughts kept bumping up against the memory of Pos, too, but I firmly steered them away just as if I had the tiller in my hands to do it. It was a memory that was only going to make me fret more than I already was. And I felt rough enough that even a straw added to the load I felt I was carrying, would indeed be upon the camel's back. I made myself some hot herbal tea, to ease my stomach or hopefully so, in the kettle set in the little efficiency with a fly-spotted mirror hung up above it. It wasn't the most flattering of mirrors, true, but I winced when I caught a glimpse of my own face in it, as I filled my vacuum flask. I didn't know if the greenish tinge was nausea, or just poor lighting, but either way I wasn't looking my best. And was that more grey in my hair than the gentle salt and pepper there'd been three months ago?

If I'd looked like this when Pos had slopped with a wave from the sea into my life, I thought ruefully, he'd probably have jumped right back overboard. I may not be the prettyboy I was once, but normally I keep myself well-groomed and cared-for. Though I might make the odd self-deprecating remark, in fact I have enough normal vanity to know that I'm a reasonably handsome fellow still, in a bony, brooding, aristocratic way. (Which is deeply misleading, since my people are bourgeois to the bone – a clan of shopkeepers, indeed. But it's a good look, and has served me well many times.)

But now, I was looking fairly seedy. I couldn't imagine how I'd managed to score with a beautiful creature like Pos in the first place, frankly.

And those were the self-pitying thoughts that were roaming about in my mind, as I settled myself down and debated putting a shot from my hipflask into my mug. They were only briefly derailed, when I heard a massive *thunk* slam down on the deck outside at the rear of the boat.

I should probably have got up and investigated immediately, hearing that. The reason that I didn't – barring sloth and fatigue and whiny sickness – was that I'd stashed a spare life-raft to the rear a couple of days ago, propped up on the outside of the hold. (Thinking that I'd move it somewhere more stable and suitable in just a moment. Which, clearly, and as we see, had not happened. Well, I hadn't been well – that was my excuse.)

I did mean to get up and check it out in just a minute or two, though. A minute or two, after I'd had a swig of tea, and rested my aching bones and back just a little longer. It occurred to me, now, that with my state of nausea, perhaps setting out on the open sea hadn't been such a brilliant idea, even though I wasn't normally one bit seasick.

Oh, poor me, poor me, that was what I was thinking, basically.

Then that got interrupted by a much quieter, gentler sound – a knock at the cabin door. A nice, quiet knock. I have never been more startled or freaked out or cold-sweating in my life. Not ever. Wouldn't you have been, too? A knock on the door, in the middle of the night. On a little boat on the Scottish seas, out of harbour, and with only one person – the cabin inhabitant – on the boat. Theoretically, in any case.

It was the very essence of every ghost story I'd ever read. The fact that it didn't give me a heart attack is probably only down to the fact that I was already feeling too lousy in a dozen different ways, for my body to concentrate on my cardiac area. I was still sitting there, though, staring wide-eyed and panicked at the door, and wondering if I'd just – hopefully – imagined it. Along with Pos, himself, perhaps, which would make me truly delusional. That would not be such good news, after all.

Except then it came again, and that was definitely, oh, yes, definitely a knock. Bloody hell. Maybe ghosts were real, after all? This felt like the worst possible time to find that out. My mouth was utterly dry, and I swallowed and wondered whether opening the door, or not opening the door, would be the worse option. Depending on what it was that was lurking and waiting outside.

Except then it wasn't only the knocking that I had to contend with. Because then the music started up – the music, by which I mean the *singing*.

And I recognised it immediately, the very second it began. It was quite unmistakable, that eerie and plaintive solo voice, that quiet, piercing, gentle plainsong. It was... Well, mostly, it was probably a very bad idea to jump up out of my chair quite as urgently and jerkily as I did, paying no mind to the fact that a) I was a bit poorly and b) the chair itself was pretty rickety. I nearly took a leg – a chair leg – off, bashing it against the side of the cabin. But I didn't care about that, right now. I leapt to the door, and wrenched it open.

So much the worse for me, if it actually had turned out to be a ghost or a grim ghoul. But I was lucky, and accurate. It was Pos, just the way I'd been certain.

And it was probably slightly pathetic, the way I had to lean a little bit against the door-frame. Partly because I felt weak at the knees at the sight of him – after all this time. And partly because, hell, I just felt a little bit weak at the knees, because I'd jumped up abruptly and I wasn't very well either. But I was stunned, and shocked, and, well... pleased to see him. Even though I probably ought to be furious, or at least overtly cool and dismissive. I ought to have a lot more pride, considering that he'd had his shockingly expert and pleasurable way with me, and then disappeared into the night with never a word of appreciation or farewell. (Very well, I wouldn't have understood any such word. But the principle, there's still the principle. That's what matters.)

It was nice that he looked just as pleased to see me. It made the whole thing a mite less embarrassing. So pleased, in fact, that he opened his arms wide, and didn't wait one moment for me to come forward and hug him – he just enveloped me in nice thick strong arms and hugged the life out of me, pretty nearly. I'd paused just that one moment to register that yes, the absolute bastard was on two legs again. (And didn't I wish he'd just make up his mind one way, or the other? Well, not so much, perhaps. There were convenient aspects to his legged form, principally located between the two of them.) That noisy, clumsy flop had to have been him coming over the side of the boat. And anything so graceless – out of the water – must have been accomplished while he was still equipped with a silvery, splashing tail. Which meant he had to be able to switch from one to the other with pretty impressive speed.

(I had to wonder, if all of the fuss and sweat difficulty of getting him into my home – into my van, even – that last time I'd seen him, had really been necessary. Perhaps he'd only been amusing himself, seeing if I could overcome the obstacle of his tail and had enough determination, and sly sexual interest, to manage to achieve the objective. Perhaps it had all been a test, which I had passed and been rewarded for. The thought made me feel like an indulged child, and slightly humiliated.)

And now I was getting a second unscheduled visit, presumably with the same end in view? Perhaps Pos thought that a human guy was an easy mark, couldn't resist his supernatural beauty, would always give in and give him anything he wanted... Which was probably true, at least in my own case. If I was honest, I'd fallen a little bit for him, even with so little time and basis for it. It made me a little foolish. I was a damn sight too old – mature – and wise, to be getting sulky over being so easily forgotten by a casual hook-up. Or I would have thought so.

But my emotions had been a mess, lately, as mercurial and unreliable as a pre-Copernican calendar or a map including the words *here be dragons* for navigating the seas. That was the excuse I chose to put forward to myself, at any rate. When I pulled away from him quite roughly, out of his arms, and stepped backwards, back into the cabin. I was pretty sure there was a sour expression on my face, too, defensive and hostile. I could feel it.

But it didn't seem to put Pos off, not a bit. He followed me right in there, grabbed me and kissed me. And he didn't let me go when I pushed at his shoulders, his chest, and frankly snarled at him. And then he did – just a moment – and threw his hands up. The expression in his eyes – damn, those eyes – was wicked. It was a come-on that he knew quite well – much too well – was strongly seductive to me. He might as well have said, if he'd had any English, 'Well, do you really mean it? I'll put you down and leave you be – if you really mean it...'

And I suppose I didn't mean it so much, after all. Because I let him draw me back into him, close against him, gently. One hundred percent naked as he was, and still wet from the sea, and seemingly feeling not much the worse for it either.

I was a grown man, mature, even middle-aged if you were feeling less than kind – and yet I rested my head on his shoulder, and nestled into the warmth of him. You could say nestled, it would be a perfectly accurate description. I felt how my chest heaved, how my breathing was urgently laboured at the shock he'd given me, and I needed the comfort. I wasn't going to try to justify it beyond that.

He held me against him, and he took my hand and held it, gently. I could hear him mumbling quietly in my ear. No doubt it was some kind of admonition not to be a terrible little sulker, see, he'd come back eventually, hadn't he? And then he began to nose around and nuzzle at me, my cheeks, neck, ears, forehead, lips. And then back around, to do the rounds again. It was like he'd been happy enough to hold me, for a few moments, but then something had alerted him. He'd sensed something that had him suddenly tense and careful and frantically active, his hands on me light but definitely holding me in place as he examined the matter further. And what the hell? *I* wasn't the one climbing on board boats in the middle of the night, bare-arse naked and accosting casual lays of my past history. I thought that, with a good deal of petulance. What the hell was the chancer playing at?

His hands strayed further, then, letting go of my shoulder, my waist. He still had a hold of me by one shoulder, but his other hand strayed down to my abdomen, grazing against it with his clean white sea-washed knuckles. Perhaps I was a bit bloated – I still felt sick as hell, though I couldn't focus on that thought much mentally, what with present distractions going on – but it wasn't exactly tactful or diplomatic of him to draw attention to it that way. I said as much, not that he was paying a bit of attention to me, or rather to anything but my belly, gazing down at it, rapt.

Then he looked back up at me, and his cheeks were more flushed than I'd seen them ever before. Normally his skin tone was a lovely marble-white, with just a faint trace of olive, and he looked like he'd just swept up out of the sea, the way he actually had. Now he was flushed with emotion, or it looked like that, and his eyes were starry-bright. "Baby!," he said to me, and I was as wise as I was before he'd said it.

I must have looked at him very expressively – and perhaps a bit exasperatedly, too. Because he grinned – eyes still wide and wet – and he straightened up, and leant to whisper in my ear. "Baby," he said, and that was a revelation. The sneaky so-and-so. I knew now, for sure, that he had at least one word of English available to him. Even if it was thickly and strangely accented, and spoken as carefully as if he thought it might damage his mouth if he did it wrong.

And he patted my belly, as if for emphasis. I laughed out loud. He was a pretty one, my man from the sea. So pretty that I hadn't realised that he was touched in the wits. "A baby," I repeated, incredulous. "You think I'm having a baby? Well, love, I suppose it's not so surprising that you're a bit deficient in the basics of human biology and anatomy, if you've got a fishy tail most of the time. I hate to break it to you, sunshine, but–"

That was the moment that the odd twitchings in my belly decided to magnify themselves by a factor of a hundred or so. If I hadn't known better myself, I would have said that that was a kick, coming from inside my belly. And Pos had to have felt it too, with his hand still resting there. The proof was him turning to me, with an even fiercer grin. "Oh, this is ridiculous," I said abruptly, pulling away a little. "Either you're ready for the funny farm, or I'm the one who's lost his wits completely – I wouldn't be surprised – and I'm just hallucinating you here in the first place. Which would actually make more sense than any other option." And I took a step further back, further away from him.

I wasn't sure that he was even listening, though. He was too busy pulling a ring off his finger – one of two, identical, but he only took one. And then he grabbed my hand, and without permission or ceremony – certainly with no going down on one knee – he manoeuvred my fingers a bit, and started to slide it onto my finger. I won't say that I exactly put up a struggle – perhaps I was too dazed for that. But I wasn't completely cooperative, either. Still, he was quick and insistent and had surprise to his advantage. And suddenly, there I was, with a ring on my finger.

A ring? Well, I didn't know for sure if it was some kind of betrothal ring. But it seemed like a reasonable conclusion to draw. Really. And it wasn't even as if it was the first time I'd been here. I'd co-habited with two men and one woman at this point. (I don't mean simultaneously, although poly is fine, I have nothing against poly. I just don't have the energy.) I'd nearly married one guy, until he'd decided his lawyer ex was a better bet for a cosy well-fed old age, and dumped me a month before the big day. I'd dated, I'd been on the scene, I'd been around.

There was no reason for my eyes to tear up as I stared down at my hand. It wasn't even all that much to look at. No big stones, no fancy setting. Just a plain band, that might have been copper or brass, was tinged a little greenish here and there, and with a red stone sunk into the metal. There was some engraving on the underside, which predictably was quite unreadable.

Or maybe there *was* reason. I had a feeling that those tears that were threatening might just be tears of rage. A casual pick-up – on my own boat! - after an unauthorised boarding. An irresistible seduction, and then springing it on me that, yes, actually he was fully equipped, ready for action, and also able to run a marathon any time he felt like it. (After conning me into labouring, sweating and dragging him into my little home. It was a wonder I hadn't irreversibly pulled a muscle.) And then, of course, being abruptly dumped, not a trace of him left behind when I woke up. It was months since I'd seen him. Months.

And now, he flipped himself over the side of my boat, once again, and thought that it was all back on. Now, he was suffering from the delusion that I was preggers with his kiddie – really, I might not be a biology teacher, but I was going to have to give him a few simple pointers, just for his future amours' sake – and that seemed to make all the difference. Enough difference, in fact, for him to put a ring on my finger. Me, practically middle-aged – well, middle-aged, in fact – greying, a tired romantically burned-out former book-store owner. Tired of trying at love, not even looking any more.

Yes, I was distinctly furious. I wrenched my hand out of his grip, and with my other hand I shoved him away from me with about as much effective force as I could manage against a younger, fitter, (prettier) man. And I was immediately occupied with trying to wrench the stupid ring off my finger, yanking at it hard enough to take the finger off with it at the same time, if I wasn't careful. Of course it was stuck, and I was cursing at the wretched thing, when Pos closed in on me, and put his arms around me. Tentatively at first, giving me a chance to batter him off again, to make it clear that I wasn't kidding around. And then with more confidence, folding me up into his arms as if I was fragile and charming and breakable and, well, lovely. Not a tired older guy who had got lucky once, and had no idea why Pos had even turned up on my doorstep – my boat-side – a second time. Why he would pursue me, all over again.

I did still have enough pride to pound ineffectively at his chest with a lax fist, not enough to hurt or to make him pull away. Just enough to make the point, that I was *very very angry* with him. And his hand closed firmly over my fist, and held it there, against his chest.

"My love?" he said. Or at least that's as near as I can get to what he said. And he bashed my fist against his chest, gently but insistently. "My dear?"

I ignored him, and just continued to sigh and mumble to myself, insults directed his way and despairing lectures my own. But he did it again, and then again. And when he was clearly about to do the same thing a fourth time, I took some notice. Elaborate signs and gestures and vigorous head-nodding can be pretty annoying, when you're beginning to suspect that someone has a lot more English than they're letting on, though. "Heart?" I guessed, my head still huddled against him, voice muffled. "You mean heart?"

And he screwed up his face, in the dim yellowish light of the stuffy little cabin, and wiggled his hand about, looking down at me and perking his eyebrows. Not exactly, I took that to mean. Getting there, no cigar, try again. He was warm to rest against, but I still felt sick, and irritable, and like it would take an awful lot of coddling before I thought about forgiving him. That was probably the reason I was little bit mean about it, why I was deliberately uncomprehending. "Chest?" I asked, and then, "Tits? Man-bosom?" Perhaps it was snide and childish, and perhaps he didn't deserve any better. (I did feel sick, I really did. That's the case for my defence.)

He squeezed me a little tighter, and I did feel admonished like a naughty child. But he also brushed his cheek up against mine, soft enough to be tender. I felt the rough graze and burr, because he needed a shave, and I smelt the sea, clean and salty. Oh, well, I thought. It wouldn't kill me to grudgingly throw him a bone, let him have a little something. "Love?" I asked, as much like a schoolteacher as I could make it.

He nodded – warm and vehement – and I made my laugh in response as cynical as I had the capacity for. "Well. Isn't that nice. You suck me off in the bath, and fuck me in my bed when you sprout a nice shiny new cock. And then you run off and leave me sleeping in bed and that's all I hear about you for weeks. No, for months. Thanks for that! And now you appropriate my bloody *boat* again, and you think I'm having your little *baby* – oh God – and suddenly it's hearts and flowers and a ring on my finger. Thanks! No thanks!"

I really did shove him away this time, with intent. And the force of it made me fall back onto the chair, which was a good thing, because I was middle-aged and tired and felt sick and my ankles were swelling, these past few days. And I was doing my best not to cry. But I was certainly as screechy and melodramatic as a jilted schoolgirl. "You can't think – you can't – this isn't acceptable – what kind of nonsense is this? Do you think I'm going to swallow this? What a stupid fairy story to spin me, how gullible you must think I am. A fine fairy story – throw a merman into it and that's the finishing touch!"

I was gulping, and I was gasping, rubbing my face where it was reddened with anger and beard-burn. Gritted-teeth vulnerability, too, maybe, but mostly anger. It should have just aggravated things, and I didn't want to soften, when he got down on his knees – his leg-based human-style knees, for as long as he decided that that was a good look – and knelt in front of me. But I breathed deeper, and got a little calmer, and let him take my hands. I didn't yank them away straight away, anyhow. Maybe I wanted to be persuaded. I let him kiss my hands, and touch my face, and kiss my cheek, and what the hell. I wasn't going to cut off my nose to spite my face. He'd made quite the impression, and I'd thought about him and missed him. I wasn't going to commit to anything more than that. But it was nice to have him there.

I was just thinking that if I could press him into service to massage my aching feet, then he'd have justified his existence and excused his misdemeanours, and I really would be ready to forgive him. That was when he reached out and touched the side of my neck, very gently. And his other hand was stroking the ring that was still on my finger, stuck and obdurate. There was no getting it off, not without butter and ice and cold water, it seemed.

Something fluttered in my neck, then – something that seemed to respond immediately and from down deep in the tissues, at his touch. I'd never felt anything like that before, and it made me jump, and quiver under his hands. And my eyes went to the same spot on him, that smooth light-olive broad thick neck, muscular as every other bit of him.

It wasn't the first time I'd seen it, but it was the first time I'd seen it quiver to life, spring up from the smooth perfect human skin. It was his gills, the ones that had been pressed into service when he'd – well, when he'd required them, with me in the bath, weeks back and more. And I touched my hand to the side of my neck, where I felt the flutter like wings or the swish of a tail, and – yes. I could feel, the same ridges and opening little mouths, the same flex and squish as they made ready, to breathe water instead of air.

Oh. Oh damn.

My eyes fixed on him, and I wasn't sure, quite, if it was in horror or in wonder. "Oh, hell," I whispered. "What have you done to me? Is it magic? Is it the damn ring?" He was still stroking the damn ring. It made me suspicious.

In reply, he gave me a little smirk that twisted up his face sideways – and he wasn't any less handsome for it, the swine – and stroked a hand down my leg, instead. (Modestly covered in canvas chinos, too, perfectly respectable. Unlike this naturist marine arsehole.) Under his hands I felt a heat and a tingle – and I couldn't absolutely say that I didn't see a momentary blur and shimmer, see my legs disappear for a second and be replaced by silver scales, long flexing muscles. By fins. By a single tail, not two legs.

I stared at him, dismayed. But maybe not as dismayed as I ought to have been. And his sea-coloured eyes gazed back, with one eyebrow raised. He touched his hand to my chest, now – and then to his. And then he pointed away from both of us – out of the cabin, out into the dark. In that direction, there wasn't the island. That was off the other way. He was pointing out to the open sea.

Go with him, that's what he was asking. Did I want to go with him? Would I come with him? He leaned in and kissed me, fast and hot and fierce, now. Quite serious, for all his kidding and play-acting up until now. His skin was hot and fiery under my lips – I kissed him back, yes, damn him – and oh, he ran hot for a sea creature.

I'd have to be crazy, I really would. What, leave behind my little cottage, and my pleasant quiet life, and the few friends I kept in touch with, and... I sounded about ninety-three in my own ears, not forty-three. As if I'd not only retired, but also expired, gradually toddling onwards to a respectable boring death.

Or on the other hand, I could take the hand of this passionate beautiful crazy supernatural creature, and leap into an adventure I couldn't know beforehand. Or dive into it, rather.

I knew what the sensible thing to do was. But even so, I took his hand, and I squeezed it. And nodded and smiled, when he looked at me in question, peering in earnestly.

I still squawked like a chicken, when he grabbed me up and ran with me, for the edge of the boat, for the dark night and the sea. Well, I hadn't reckoned on anything quite so abrupt. But the actual physical materialization of the tail he'd visually promised me, the gills flexing ready for water in my neck, they distracted me as he leapt up to the side of the boat.

As he dived with me, down into the deep, deep deep down, suddenly tailed and gilled himself, two men of the sea in the waters so very deep.

But what about my *boat*, I thought. And it was my last thought in human form.

• • • •

OF COURSE THAT WASN't the end of the story, not from my angle. Down in the sea, in a new form and a new life, I found out the reasons why my pretty merman had disappeared out of my life for so long, when we'd had such a flirty and beguiling beginning. Because I'd called him a prince, before now, but only in a snide way, in the most caustic manner possible. Except, more fool me, with all the facts assembled. He actually *was* – and his father, the king, wasn't especially thrilled by him diving home after an adventure on heathen dry land, and announcing himself in love with one of the two-legged malformed folk. And how about if he brought a husband home next time he went adventuring?

It had led to many a merry old row, and cursings and disownings and dragging back home. At least until my Prince Pos – no, not his real name, but it was stuck for me, by now – had hammered out an agreement about duties and dominions and borders and whatnot, and been handed over his birthright undersea lands and given blessing to go find his one true mate. (!) Oh, and given many assurances, apparently, of his prospective spouse's fertility, and suitability to provide the kingdom with many fine healthy heirs. Lying through his teeth all the while, because even the eyes of love, looking at me, wouldn't consider me an obvious prospect for mating and breeding.

Except then, he did come to find me, and there I was. With my belly puffed out, and a list of symptoms that any expectant mother would run through sorrowfully, nodding her head. But how was I to know? I'd joked about it – but who would have thought that the seafolk thought male pregnancy the most natural and everyday occurrence in the world? (Even for a human seduced into adopting their form, running off with an aristocratic merman lover, and giving birth to his sweet little fishy babies?)

It was a shock. I'm not going to deny it, and say that it wasn't. And not simply by reason of being, well, a male of the human species, obviously. Quite apart from that, I was... not quite still in my prime. Who expects to suddenly become a parent, and a biological parent, even, at my age?

And yet now, with my baby in my arms, in a glass and crystal underwater palace and looking out onto the far distant marine prairies, I can't claim to be sorry about it. My babies make up for everything – my babies, and my Poseidon, my man of the sea. Who comes up behind me, tail flexing and swinging, and slides a hand over my belly. My swollen belly, where it's already full with my second pregnancy, damn the uxorious fertile sexy sea-monster that he is.

He points out to the far coral gardens, where the other three of our litter of infants are playing, tails swinging in the tides. And he calls out a warning, when one of them is about to fall over a playful seahorse and into a multi-coloured fountain out of a deep, deep volcano of the ocean. For why, yes, multiple births are common amongst the seafolk, it has turned out. Although they're live births, and not the laying of eggs as if we were actual *fish*. That would have been a little alarming to me, even given all the new developments and surprising explorations that I've managed to absorb and accept.

I lean back against him, against my virile young love, and I think about how much he's brought to me, how he's lit up my life with so much beauty. Racing each other in the sea, silver-blue tails flashing like oily quicksilver. Playing with our children and looking forward to the new litter, walking in crystal halls that shimmer with an unearthly charm. And, when the fancy takes us, returning on two legs each, us and the kids, to re-visit my little earthly home, and go out sailing on the little boat that's responsible for so much.

I feel the kiss he presses to my ear, and the urgency of his desire and pleasure as his tail presses against me and promises other forms and other consummations, writhing pleasures of the royal marriage bed. "Darling," he murmurs, and he has enough English now, of his own and taught by me, to promise me many things. And for me to even understand, when he does so.

It's a joyful day, every day here for me in this underwater kingdom. And I hold on to him tightly, and try not to think about the fact that his mother and father, the king and queen to our two princes of the realm, are expecting our presence at the royal merfolk banquet, in their great sea-palace tonight.

Even underwater, everyone meets with a little trouble sometimes, the odd dark cloud, a drop of rain here and there. And royal in-laws – even merfolk royal in-laws – are one of the troubles, the clouds.

I sigh, and kiss his hand, my Pos. And then I dive off into the blue shadows of the water, tail flipping side to side, and let him hunt and chase me in the depths of the sea.

. . . .

END